P9-DMR-878

# Clifford THE BIG RED DOG®

# THE BIGGEST EASTER EGG

by Sonia Sander

Illustrated by The Artifact Group

Based on the Scholastic book series
"Clifford The Big Red Dog"
by Norman Bridwell

ISBN 0-439-78954-0

Designed by Michael Massen

12  11  10  9  8  7  6  5  4  3  2          07  08  09  10

Printed in the U.S.A.
First printing, February 2006

## SCHOLASTIC INC.

New York      Toronto      London      Auckland      Sydney
Mexico City      New Delhi      Hong Kong      Buenos Aires

"Look, Clifford!" said Emily Elizabeth.

"We are painting eggs!"

"*Woof!*" barked Clifford.

"That's right, boy," said Emily Elizabeth.
"Easter is almost here."

Clifford loved Easter!

He wanted to paint an egg, too.

First, he needed to find an egg.

With Cleo and T-Bone's help,
Clifford looked all over the farm
for just the right egg to decorate.

"How about a chicken egg just like Emily Elizabeth's?" asked Cleo.

Clifford thought that was a good idea,
but the egg was too small for him.

"Look, Clifford," said T-Bone.

"Charlie is using a turtle egg.

That is bigger than a chicken egg."

So Clifford and his friends
went to look for a turtle egg.

It didn't take long before Clifford and his friends tracked down Mama Turtle.

She said Clifford could borrow one of her eggs as long as he promised to bring it back. "I promise," said Clifford.

The new egg was a little easier to paint.
But as Clifford tried to add stickers
to his egg, the baby turtle hatched!

"Mama!" cried the turtle.

"Oh, no, the baby turtle thinks Clifford is his mama," said Cleo.

"I'm not your mother," said Clifford.
"Your mother lives over there,
on the riverbank."

But the baby turtle didn't believe Clifford.

So Clifford gave the baby turtle a ride

back to his mother.

Clifford was ready to give up,
but Cleo and T-Bone wouldn't let him.
"We found our perfect egg,"
said Cleo and T-Bone. "You can, too!"

Clifford and his friends made
one more pass around the farm.

"Look!" called T-Bone.

"It's a great big ostrich egg.

That is perfect for Clifford!"

T-Bone was right.

Luckily, Mama Ostrich
wanted to take a walk.

She was more than happy
to lend her egg to Clifford
while she was gone.

Clifford and his friends
moved the egg very carefully.

"Easy does it," said Clifford.

"Not too fast, now."

Before long, Clifford was
hard at work on his egg.

This time, he had no problem
painting his Easter egg.

"Ta-da!" shouted Clifford.

"What do you think?"

Mama Ostrich loved
her newly painted egg.

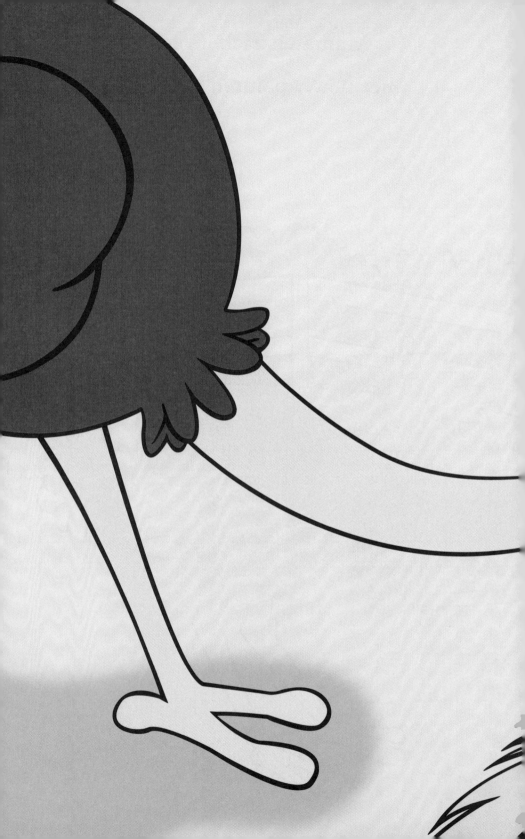

She proudly sat on her egg
until it hatched.

She didn't have to wait long!

*Crack! Crack!*

Clifford was a little sad to see his egg crack. But he soon saw that if he held his egg just so, it looked almost as good as new.

It was a very happy Easter for Clifford and all his newly hatched friends!

# Do You Remember?

**Circle the right answer.**

1. What was Clifford trying to do when the turtle egg hatched?

   a. Paint the egg.

   b. Add stickers to the egg.

   c. Find a new egg.

2. Who saw the ostrich egg first?

   a. Cleo

   b. Clifford

   c. T-Bone

**Which happened first?**

**Which happened next?**

**Which happened last?**

**Write a 1, 2, or 3 on the line after each sentence.**

Clifford paints the perfect egg. _____

The ostrich egg hatches. _____

Mama Turtle lends her egg to Clifford. _____

**Answers:**